Lou C. Wright

Fairy Tale

Fairy Tale

Erich Segal

Drawings by Dino Kotopoulis

HARPER & ROW, PUBLISHERS

New York, Evanston, San Francisco, London

FIRST EDITION

STANDARD BOOK NUMBER: 06–013828–9

LIBRARY OF CONGRESS CATALOG CARD NUMBER: 72–9101

Designed by Patricia Dunbar

For Jeremy, Kathy, Jed & Erich
and Trebbe

Once upon a time—

or maybe twice—

a thing happened.

A nice thing

Atip the top of an obscure Ozark in a quaint little settlement known as Poop's Peak there dwelt and lived a group of hardy mountaineers. They were steeped in the traditions of their forefathers. Or rather, soaked in them. From generation to generation, the Poopers had zealously clung to the truths which made them free. Namely, snoozing and boozing. The latter provided their one and only livelihood. For the Poopers were congenital shiners of moon, which is to say, hootch hustlers, which is to say, distillers of illegal whiskey. Moreover, they quite often polished what they shined. Actually, the product of this unknown region was not unknown in regions beyond; Poop's Peak supplied some ten percent of all the likker sold in Euphoria County. Many notables swore by it. Especially when under the influence of it.

In the very heart or, better said, the very liver of Poop's Peak dwelt the clan of Kertuffel, whose leader, chief operating officer and father was Ezekiel. Ezekiel ("Zeke") ran a still of distinction. It was known and acknowledged up and down the Peak that Zeke was best of all possible moonshiners. The skill of his still gave a thrill to the swill. Good stuff, and tasty, too. In fact, unbeknownst to Zeke or the clan, a bottle of Kertuffel Kool, unscrupulously labeled Loch Ness

Nectar, was awarded the Grand Prix du Scotch at the 1880 World's Fair in Paris, Kentucky. Of course that brew was Granddaddy Zeb's brewing, but clan-folk would never amend the blend, so Zeke's potion differed not one iota from that beverage pseudony-mously honored at the Paris Fair. Well, Zeke never paid any heed to anything 'cepting sales and sales were good. In fact, the Kertuffels were the affluentest folks in Poop's Peak and surrounding areas.

Not only were they affluent,

they were also

wealthy and rich.

Zeke had more than seventy-eight dollars invested in his mattress, and at least two dollars more in small change which he used to buy Cokes and things whenever the family was out on an excursion in their old Model T, whether 'round Poop's Peak, Mount Mungo or other metropolitan areas nearby. For, contrary to popular belief, not everyone nowadays barters. Which is to say, not everyone trades *his* wares for *your* wares. Like Zeke would exchange with surrounding tillers of the earth hootch for hay or booze for broccoli. All of this supplies the economic background for our story.

Which has nothing to do with Coke machines, but much to do with the obsolescence of bartering in advanced cultures and its replacement by a money economy. Also, there is the matter of conspicuous consumption, a notion put forth by the great Professor Thorstein Veblen (1857–1929), who never tasted Kertuffel Kool, but whose name and theory have considerable relevance—and add considerable luster—to this tale. Which is to say, the Kertuffels felt an ever-increasing desire to peacock their success to the community at large. To be pacesetters and fulfillers of the American Dream. This marks the end of the speculative, conjectural and hypothetical section and we return to a simpler mode of expression.

One bright morn,

Zeke called a meeting

of the clan.

When all were gathered, he made an oration-type speech which all found eloquent, moving, dignified, persuasive and fitfully even coherent. It did not befit, said Zeke, nor did it behoove either, the most abundant family in the Peak to drive about in their antiquated Model T. Actually, Zeke did not employ the term "antiquated," inasmuch as it was not a term either congenial or familiar to his usual parlance. Rather, he used terminology like "hunk" and "heap" and "wreck" in monosyllabic reference to the old-fangledness of the vehicle which had been transporting the Kertuffel clan since the earliest Model T-times. The buckshot of Zeke's oration-speech was that the clan should get theirselves a newer thang, a classier, snazzier, zippier model. Perhaps even one with a top. Where were such wonders obtainable? Surely not in the surrounding or even outlying areas. Cars of such advanced complexity existed only in places like the Big City. Thus and ergo, someone had to go to the Big City and barter the Model T for something groovier and, as it were, behoovier.

Zeke, no fool he, was well aware that he might have to throw some mattress money into the bargain as well. But whom to entrust with this automobilization? The choice narrowed quickly down to Zeke's favorite son. He was a lad wise beyond his years, quick of wit, of hand and eye, a man of the world and a cool customer, for the Kertuffels were in fact about to assume the status of customer. Also, it did not escape the keen mind of Zeke Kertuffel that son Jake, age seventeen, was the only member of the family who could read.

We cannot here relate how it came to pass that Jake Kertuffel mastered the alphabet and once even scored a near-perfect 24 on an A-B-C test. All this has to do with Jake's having spent some time in a school (as you probably guessed), and those adventures will have to wait for another time's tell-

ing. In any case, on the next morning, which by coincidence also turned out to be bright and early, Jake Kertuffel bade farewell to his father, his mother, his seventeen brothers and sisters, his cousins and aunts, leapt (or leaped—I forget which) into the Model T and chugged off down the long and winding road which led from Poop's Peak . . . ultimately . . . to the Big City.

The Big City! Imagine young Jake in the Big City, hopes high, pockets full, nose clean, and the Model T in third gear. What a thrill—even for us as we hear it retold.

Neon! Neon at noon! Yes, believe it or not, right on Main Street there was lighted Neon at Noon! It might even have been there earlier, but noon was when Jake arrived and noon was when he spied the fuzzy-pink electric sign bleating

Scattered around in very near vicinity of the sign were some three dozen motorcars of varying hues and differing colors. Jake made an educated guess (worthy of his aforementioned education) that Happy Humphrey must be in the business of selling these cars. And so he turned his sputtery, now-tired (and soon to be re-tired) auto into Happy Humphrey's lot.

Happy
Humphrey

sat in his hut.

The hut was in the center of his lot. The sort of lot which served as office by day and sleep house by night. Being that it was noon, Happy Humphrey, a jolly rotund fellow of lower middle age, was eating. Specifically, he was eating a pork chop. Between munches, Happy Humphrey looked out onto the lot. There he saw this very strange and odd-looking auto stagger to a stop. As you probably guessed, it was Jake. Frankly, Happy Humphrey was somewhat annoyed to be distracted from the munch of his lunch, but nevertheless he wiped his greasy hands on his trousers and walked to meet the barefoot lad, who had carefully cleaned and polished his feet for the occasion.

Jake shook what turned out to be the not-too-tidy hand of Happy Humphrey and then took verbal initiative as well:

"We'd like to trade this here car for a new one," he said. For a rural lad he was forceful and very articulate.

"Aha," said Happy Humphrey. "Aha" is what he said, but in his heart he was thinking something quite different. In his heart, Happy Humphrey was thinking, "Oho." For his shrewd and beady eyes at once recognized that the vehicle Jake had arrived in was none other than the rare and all but nonexistent Model T-4-2, a collector's item for which collectors would pay astrodomical sums. Which is why he said, "Oho."

To himself, that is.

"Son, that old heap ain't worth a pile of beans," chortled Happy Humphrey to Jake Kertuffel, and I don't have to tell you he was lying through his tooth. "Certainly, son," he continued, "it ain't worth a whole entire new—which is to say—other car."

"Oh," said Jake, saddened by Happy Humphrey's sober statement. But he persisted.

"Ah also have twenty dollars, suh," said Jake. It will be noted that, country boy that he was, Jake was nonetheless couth and polite and would even say "suh" to a swine like Happy Humphrey. He withdrew a tattered twenty from his tattered trousers.

"I'll take it," said Humphrey, taking it. His jowls flapped in the noonday breeze as he stood there thinking tricky thoughts about how further to fleece this innocent from the far-off hills.

"What kind o' car can I git?" asked Jake.

"Car???" said Happy Humphrey. His voice was nasal and scrapy. "You all expect an entire car jus' for twenty bucks and a vehikul that ain't worth but a pile o' beans?"

Jake now felt kind of sorry he had asked.

"Well, what can I git, suh?" he inquired.

"A pile of beans," said Happy Humphrey.

Jake was puzzled by this reply, as, no doubt, are many readers. Herewith, however, comes the explanation. In Happy Humphrey's hut there was a desk. In the bottom drawer of this desk there were some paper clips, slightly pre-used chewing gum and some beans. They looked like wrinkled lima beans.

"What are they?" Happy Humphrey had asked Juicy Jeremy, from whom he had long ago bought the desk (cheap). "Oh, jus' some wrinkled lima beans," Juicy Jeremy replied and gifted them to Happy Humphrey along with the rest of the contents of the drawer. Happy Humphrey had always intended to cook up these beans for a Sunday supper, but somehow years passed and the notion got ever less appealing. Here now was a chance for Happy Humphrey to dispose of Juicy Jeremy's crinkled limas, and to pull a fast one, hoodwink a hick, and be generally the nasty fellow he had always dreamed of growing up to become. He waddled to his hut and returned with the desiccated little dots clutched in his greasy paw.

"Here," said Happy Humphrey, offering the beans to a puzzled Jake.

"No, thankee, suh, I'm not hungry," said Jake.

"Hungry?? Ho ho ho!" said Happy Humphrey and the folds of his belly just wrinkled like jelly. "Why, son, you don't *eat* these. These are magic beans."

"Magic beans?"

A thrill ran up Jake's spine as no doubt it is now ascending the spine of many a reader.

Magic beans, the stuff

that dreams are made of!

And also magic

vegetable stew.

Magic beans! The mind pirouettes with fantasies of purple moonbeams, silver confetti and stereophonic lollipops!

And how could poor Jake Kertuffel, whose first trip this was to the Big City, how could he know that you never buy magic beans in a used-car lot! Much less from a huffing hunk of hollow hilarity like Happy Humphrey!

Not that Jake didn't make one or two probing comments. Like, "It sure doesn't look like a car, suh." (For an instant he had recalled the injunction of Papa Zeke.) Jake's perspicacity was a credit to Mrs. Vilma Vacancy ("Marm"), his long-ago schoolteacher.

For a moment Happy Humphrey was off guard. He was unaccustomed to this kind of piercing repartee. "But," he spoke up, swiftly regaining his villainous power of dialectic, "you can't *plant* a car!"

"Oh," said Jake, somewhat awed by a verity which was coincidentally true.

"But these beans are *made* for plantin'," Happy Humphrey added.

Which, you must admit, is a pretty creative reply. And Happy Humphrey had driven home his point. Which is more than Jake would be able to do with the beans.

There was a pause.

"What happens then?" Jake queried.

"Just plant and wait," said Happy Humphrey, who was stalling for time, all the while rummaging his pea-pod brain for some kind of flim with which to flam young Jake. Then from a tiny crevice of his mind, he recalled a bedtime story told very, very long ago by Huge Hilda, his mother. And he foisted the fable onto Jake as if it were true, which is the kind of behavior that gives bedtime stories a bad name.

"You all plant these magic beans in yo' garden. You all tend them and defend them with water like you orter. Then, if the moon is high and the wind is nigh and the corn is as spry as an elephant's thigh—"

"What then, Happy Humphrey???"

Happy Humphrey had temporarily run out of rhymes. "I dunno, son, but the folk tale says then a *money tree* will grow."

"A money tree??? But money doesn't grow on trees, Mr. Happy Humphrey, suh," said Jake, not knowing much about money but having a lifelong acquaintance with trees. Yet the thought gave cause for reflection.

"Could I have time to reflect a whit, Mr. Happy Humphrey, suh?" said Jake.

"Ho ho ho," replied Happy Humphrey (which was not quite dialectical), and quick as a wink he zipped a piece of paper from his pocket.

"What's that piece of paper you jus' zipped from your pocket, suh?" Jake asked.

"A contrack," said Happy Humphrey. "Why don't you sign? Cain't you write?"

Write??! The sudden affront to Mrs. Vilma Vacancy ("Marm")'s erstwhile semi-prize pupil cut him to the quickly.

"Sure I can write," he said proudly. And to prove it, he signed his name on the dotted line with the stubby pencil provided by the Merchant of Fenders himself. Before he could blink, Happy Humphrey had rezipped the paper into his pocket, scrunched the wrinkled beans into Jake's hand and begun to waddle hutward.

"Say, Mr. Happy Humphrey, suh," said Jake.

"Yes, son?" said Happy Humphrey, turning but still back-waddling hutward.

"What are we gonna do without a car???"

"Now, son," said Happy Humphrey in admonitory tones, "conquer your obsession with material things!"

And before you could recite the entire alphabet,
Happy Humphrey had disappeared in a cloud of dirt.
Actually, he had bolted his hut door and hidden under
the desk.

Jake was bewildered. Here he was minus car and
cash, and all for a handful of beans. How would he
even get home? What would he say to Papa Zeke?
Well, he'd figure something out during the long
trudge back to Pooperland.

Two days. It took two days to trudge back to
Poop's Peak, stopping only to snooze fitfully and eat
what berries he could find. It was a bright and early
morn when he arrived.

"Whar's the car?" asked Lemuel, one of his many
brothers. In a flash, the rest of the family were
mustered on the porch.

"Whar's the car?" they asked in choral unison.

Then Zeke himself appeared and asked the same
question: "Whar's the car?"

Then Jake told the tale of the magic beans.

And then—luckily—Lemuel's rifle jammed, or the
conversation would have ended abruptly.

"Okay," said Zeke a while later. "Sit down and tell me about it."

"I cain't sit down, Paw."

"Oh, yeah. Well, turn yer hide to the wind and tell me standin' up."

The tale did not improve in its second telling. Only this time, Zeke berated not only his scion but his self, and not just for letting Jake go to the City, but for letting him go—even for that brief spell—to a school. "This here's a hundred-proof proof that book larning don't do no one no good!"

The punishment was that Jake would go on half salary (twenty-five cents a week) till the cost of a coupe was recouped. That would be roughly around four hundred years.

"And throw away them gol-darn foolish beans," said Zeke and he stomped off.

But Jake, despondent, disconsolate, discouraged and dispirited, was nonetheless not dissuaded. In a secret nook of a secret cranny in a secret corner of the Kertuffel back yard in Poop's Peak, he planted the beans. The rest is history.

Or more precisely,

fairy tale.

Day in and day out (and vice versa), whatever time young Jake could steal from the still he would spend in the care of the bean plot. Water, sun, air, nothing was too good for them. But on the other hand, nothing seemed to be the net result. Days rolled into weeks, and though his faith never flagged, the razzing of his brothers increased to the point where Jake Kertuffel began entertaining desperate thoughts like going back to school. Or becoming an astronaut. This is the saddest part of the story, and fortunately for all concerned it ended one particular morning which somehow seemed brighter and earlier than all the others.

The revenuers came.

Traditionally, there was some sort of subtle warning about the raids of federal agents. For example, the chief would appear a few days early to visit and chat and perhaps take a few hundred gallons home as a souvenir. But unbeknownst to the mountaineers, the chief had retired last year and been replaced by some young feller who was unaware of the local traditions. This time, Poop's was caught by surprise. Hither and thither, helter and skelter they hastened to disguise, dispose of and otherwise dismantle any evidence that might suggest the illegal manufacture of alcoholic beverages. Mostly they threw the stuff in the river. (Which caused a funny incident at a church picnic downstream.) Near the Kertuffel household, the thundering hoofbeats of approaching agents grew louder. Actually, they came by car, but their engine needed retuning, so it sounded like hoofbeats. Splish and splash, every drip and drop and even the vaguest moist mist was tossed into the swirling stream. The agents arrived. Rusty doors squeaked open. Badges blinked in early-morning brightness. They found the Kertuffel clan munching peanut butter crackers on the porch. Not even a milk bottle in sight.

Oh, no? Then what was that little glint on the far side of the porch? Only Jake noticed, but it was —to use a fancy expression—crystal clearly a bottle. Of booze. Indubitably, it was a bottle of booze. Or better said, considering the circumstances, a passport to prison. But Jake popped up, leaped over, grabbed, rolled, bounced and sprinted. With the revenuers in hot pursuit (it was, as aforementioned, a sunny day), he raced across the garden toward the river. The agents were shouting things like "Stop in the name of the law," and "Hold it, kiddo," and "Gosh, I'm out of shape" as they galloped across the garden like predatory beasts. Jake, their prey—to continue the manner of speaking—despaired of reaching the river in time. So, as he ran, he uncorked the bottle with the idea of spilling its contents onto the ground. But he skipped, he tripped, the open bottle flew from his hands and landed—as fate would have it—in the very nook, the precise cranny, where long ago the magic (hah) beans had been planted. It splintered into a thousand shiny fragments and sprinkled earthward in the bright—as aforementioned—morning air.

Jake was unhurt; the evidence was nowhere in evidence and the revenuers apologized for interrupting breakfast. Zeke invited them all for peanut butter crackers, but they had to press on, for the law never rests, or even eats. And as one of the winded pursuers of young Jake was heard to remark, "I gotta get me a beer."

Redemption. Jake was redeemed. His act of valor won him dispensation from all, praise from his sisters and brothers and cousins and aunts, and the full restoration of his salary from Papa Zeke. But that is only the beginning of the story. Guess what else happened that night.

Or more exactly, guess what Jake Kertuffel noticed the next morning. Something had begun to sprout in that well-irrigated corner of the garden whither bottle had shattered and booze had rained. What sprouted was a sprout. There is no other word for it, for it was only a few inches high, though perceptibly green in the bright morning air.

Instinctively, Jake realized what had catalyzed the surgence. It was as if Moses, instead of striking the rock, had pounded on the counter of a Sinai bar. Hootch saveth. Hallelujah. Needless to say, Jake dug up some Kertuffel Kool and watered the plantlet with love and devotion. By the third day, it was two feet high—no longer a sprout, but an apprentice arbor, a tree in training! Little buds now began to appear at the end of the branches. By now, Jake was unable to sleep the night through. By 3 A.M. of the fourth day he was out in the garden, waiting for the sun to come out. It did—and precisely at sunrise too.

His shouting awakened the clan.

It worked, by jingo!

By jingo, it worked!"

In a split instant, father, mother, seventeen brothers and sisters, cousins and aunts had stampeded into the yard. Sure enough, verily and in point of true fact, on one tiny branch the little tree had produced a perfect one-dollar bill. In fact, more than perfect, for George Washington was smiling broadly, as if he knew the jubilation he was bringing to the folks in Poop's Peak.

"Look, Paw," said Jake proudly.

"I see, son," said Zeke, both proud and ashamed, since he now regretted his incredulity and ill treatment of the lad. He plucked the bill.

"It's yours, boy," he said, handing it to Jake. "You deserve it."

Jake smiled. And blushed. "Shucks" was all he said. But they knew what he meant.

By nightfall six more bills had appeared and were harvested. The tree was looking better and better, and so were the leaves. That silly grin was off George Washington's face. By the next day, the treelet was still taller and the day's growings were seventeen leaves. Zeke went out and bought shoes for all. He also declared an official Kertuffel jubilation day which would feature a barrel of 1880 Kool hid up in a cave for just such an unlikely occasion. That night the festivities began.

Three days later they ended. When the clan awoke,

their back yard was literally littered with money. By actual count there were two hundred and sixty-eight dollars—and heaven knows how much the goat had had time to consume during those blissful days of whooping up and down.

Thereafter the Kertuffel still was still. It was indeed the American Dream come true. The days melted slow and easy as whipped cream on peach-blossom pancakes. The nightly harvesting began to lose the aura of an event and became a normal chore like fetching the water or sweeping the porch. Within two weeks the entire woodshed was filled to overflow with the bloom of money. Jake, chosen bookkeeper for his aforementioned gifts of literacy, estimated the total to be in the neighborhood of fifteen thousand dollars. Who could be sure? They had long since run out of toes to aid the count and all was now conjecture. Pretty soon there would be no more room in the shed. What would they do about storing the money then?

Indeed, what would they do with it at all? Another meeting was summoned to arrive at a plan of action. The meeting was restricted to Kertuffels and cannot be reported. The results can, however, and fill the fluent paragraphs which follow.

Happy Humphrey sat in his hut, eating a Milky Way.

He looked out onto the lot and what did he see? A customer. But a very unlikely customer. It was a young lad about seventeen or so in brand-new overalls and Thom McAn shoes. Nothing unlikely about that, except that the lad was perusing a powder-blue Cadillac limousine.

Perhaps you wonder why Happy Humphrey did not quake with fear at the sight of Jake Kertuffel. Well, to wonder is to show you know very little about the mentality of crooks, or at least petty crooks. For Happy Humphrey was a cheater of people the way you and I are breathers of air. How could he keep track of the dopes he duped? Bad enough he didn't keep track of those he just plain foxed out of cash and fobbed croaky and creaky machinery onto. Still worse, he had paid no heed the previous week to the fact that the feller from Washington, D.C., who bought three rheumatic Corvairs was named R. Nader (and that's another story).

Happy Humphrey couldn't even recall his most fantastical con jobs. Not even the ninety-year-old old-maid schoolteacher whom he encouraged to trade a 1950 Kaiser-Fraser for what Happy Humphrey called "Flying Potato Chips." Actually, the old lady was quite content and never took the Potato Chips out of the garage, not even to go to church on Sunday. But no matter, that was last month and it was already phased out of Happy Humphrey's pea-sized brain.

Which is why he didn't recognize Jake Kertuffel. Or else he would not have chuckled as he watched Jake study the Caddy.

"You all don't want that one, sonny," laughed Happy Humphrey, "that's seven thousand dollars. Har har." The extra chuckle was for emphasis.

"Well," said Jake, unperturbed, "it looks like it'd hold a heap o' people. Guess'n I'll take it."

He looked at Happy Humphrey, expecting the merchant to be pleased.

"Har har," said Happy Humphrey. "Pass on, boy," he added, "and don't smudge my limo with yer fingers."

"It'll be *my* limo in a minute, by jingo," said Jake. And he stepped off the lot and called down the street, "Come on with the money, Lem!"

Lemuel Kertuffel hove into view, hauling a gunny-

sack which was really, as we know, a money sack. The brothers proceeded to empty the contents onto the ground. Happy Humphrey dropped his Milky Way.

"Where did you get that . . . that . . . er . . . stuff???" he gasped.

"Why, you oughta know, thank you very much, Mr. Happy Humphrey, suh," said Jake with a smile. "It's all yer doing, you and your magic beans."

As aforementioned, magic beans, flying potato chips and even golden-egg-laying parakeets are all part of a day's con for a sneak like Happy Humphrey. Surely this lad was trying to fool him. Perhaps the cash was even counterfeit. He held a bill to the sky and scrutinized. His shrewd if beady eye assured him it was real. That was George Washington all right and these hick yokel hayseeds appeared to have dozens, nay hundreds, nay thousands of his likeness in their sack.

"Come on into my hut, friends," he said.

He offered them—and they accepted—a soda pop (one to share) and he counted out nine thousand one-dollar bills.

"Seven thousand dollars on the nose," he said, lying through his tooth. "The rest is your change." With plenteous regret, he stuffed a few bills back into the sack. "The pop was on the hut," he added.

Zoom!

Zoom is the sound of a new used powder-blue
Cadillac zooming through the Ozarks, climbing
smoothly toward the cloud-kissed cap of Poop's
Peak. Jake and Lem took turns zooming and the hills
were alive with the sound. Needless to say, they were
elated and euphoric as well as very happy. Therefore
it is understandable that they failed to notice an in-
termittent—if distant—*vroom vroom* interspersed with
the sounds of zoom with which the hills were alive.
This was in fact the vroom of the black Thunderbird
of Happy Humphrey following the brothers at what
he shrewdly calculated to be a safe distance. We are
coming to a very dramatic part of the story. As you
probably guessed.

Surprisingly, the Caddy was only the second point
of interest at the Poopers' shack. For something rich
and strange had occurred in the brothers' absence.
Wonder of horticulture—the tree had grown further.
What is more, its foliage no longer consisted of one-
dollar bills. For now the solemn visage of Abraham
Lincoln graced the notes which grew from the tree
which rose from the beans which Happy Humphrey
gave to Jake at the very beginning. As we should recall. Today's crop alone totaled—and this is a hazy
approximation—more than twenty thousand dollars.
Poor Jake shuddered at the potential, perhaps im-

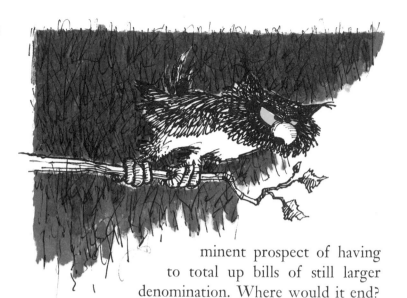

minent prospect of having to total up bills of still larger denomination. Where would it end?

But why think of tomorrow's problems? They clambered into the limo and took a quick zoom around the Peak. Needless to say, the Poopers were stunned and amazed. The Kertuffels were fulfilled. And since they had been conspicuous, they would now be consumptive. Zeke declared another shindig and they rolled out a barrel from yet another cave. They sang and danced the livelong day and the long-lived night. And, as it happened, slowly fell fast asleep.

The owl gave a hoot. At that hour he was the only one who did. After all, who else would be awake in the still—as it were—of the night?

You know who: who-ooo-ooo . . .

In the Kertuffel back yard, the money tree rustled in the midnight breeze. Beyond, there was a creak at the fence. A croaky creak, actually. It was Happy Humphrey straining to hoist over his hulk.

All afternoon he had watched in utter amazement as money was harvested, gathered and counted. He was eye-witness, beady-eye-witness, to the fact that money really could grow on trees. On one tree anyway. *He had to have that tree.* Think of what he'd become! A big man in the Big City. No more car-hustling con jobs for him! He would be wining and dining all sorts of lovelies at the "22" Club (it was a *very* Big City). It all lay before him: splendor in the grasp.

This was the philosophical part of our story. It didn't say anything anyone didn't already know. But of course, that is what philosophy is.

To the action: Happy Humphrey wanted that tree. Never you mind that it was private property or that it was fair-traded for twenty dollars and a Model T-4-2 for which he had already reaped much profit from a car fetishist in Dallas. Happy Humphrey lusted for the American Dream. And never you mind whose.

The next part

of our story

is very tense.

Late. Very. Very late. That is when most dastardly deeds take place, in the very lateness of night. There was a crescent moon. The clan of Kertuffel was sleeping. Snores in antiphonal chorus attested to this. Slack was the shack from the front to the back. This was Happy's Big Chance. For the Big Time.

Happy Humphrey clumbered over the fence onto the verdant turf. He was in. In the yard. The back yard of Ezekiel Kertuffel where grew the magical mythical wonderful tree. He crept. Stealthily. Stealthily toward the greening of the miracle. Another owl (cousin of the first) let out a hoot. Happy Humphrey froze in terror and remained so for over an hour. As aforementioned, this part is very tense. But finally Happy Humphrey moved. Toward the tree. Drooling. He was there. Imagine the thrill of being so close to a money tree you could touch it. He touched it. He even caressed it and kissed it.

But this was no time for relationships. It was a time for evil and criminal action. To wit: Happy Humphrey withdrew a minuscule ax (carried always in case of nefarious need) and, even while caressing the treelet with one hand, began to chop with the other. Chip-chop. Chip-chop. At this point it would be well to interject that as of now in America trees do not enjoy full civil rights as do horses, cats and children. Thus the full and profoundly murderous scope of Happy Humphrey's deed could not be prose-

cuted to the fullest extent in, for example, the Su-
preme Court. Furthermore, I regret to report that at
3:48 A.M. the little tree fell victim to the blows of
the ax of Happy Humphrey, Merchant of Fenders.
Sympathizers are here sanctioned to weep.

He snatched up the tree, galumphed ecstatically
toward his car and crumpled in. He was safe. What
a tragic turn of events, Happy Humphrey safe! He
vroom-vroomed into the night, jowls afloat in the
breeze.

> O Thunderbirds, now droop your wings,
> The shock absorbing all your springs,
> With such an ache
> A heart can brake.
> Why did you let a villain climb aboard?
> O golly! Gosh! O Gee! O Henry Ford!!

The magic tree was cut, in the very prime of life.
Or at least at a prime rate. More tragic still, Happy
Humphrey laughed. The wicked have no shame. And
he squooshed the accelerator and vroom-vroomed
down the long and winding road which led from
Poop's Peak—ultimately—to the Big City.

The next morning was neither bright nor early, but
it arrived nonetheless. But whereas the clanfolk knew
right off the weather was bad (a perception empiri-
cally arrived at upon seeing Lemuel drenched with
rain after he stepped off the porch), they really did

not notice the tree's absence till evening harvest time. For the record, it was tiny Gooey Kertuffel, age five and a half, who first informed his paw that the tree was gone.

"The tree's gone, Paw," he said.

And Zeke, after a rapid fact-finding field trip in the rain, verified the statement. Tiny Gooey had seen straight; the tree was indeed gone.

Sackcloth and ashes would normally be the reaction—but only in economically advanced cultures. Poop's Peak was not such a milieu and the sudden disappearance of magic money was taken with equanimity. "That's the way the tree tumbles" was one observation. Probably Jake's since he was the learnedest, and was also glad to retire as bookkeeper to return to snoozing and boozing. That part was well past. Moreover, Zeke himself had a plan to dispel whatever gloom might be glooming the Poopers.

"Wal," he said, "we got us a woodshedful o' greenbacks already. We kin get ourselves a mag-nolia tree. And mag-nolia's a durn sight prettier than money."

The folks assented, agreed and nodded yep. And actually they got several pretty new trees, including magnolia, pear (with resident partridge), as well as watermelon. So the net result was, in a way, treemendous. Also—and no small thing this—they lived happily ever after. Or at least they lived happily from that time till this time, which means from long ago to only yesterday. Heck, no one can predict the joys to come. We can just be grateful for what's been sent our way.

I know you all want to learn the fate of the flim-flamming fat man. As you surely should have inferred and surmised, Happy Humphrey did *not* live happily ever after. In fact, he lived terribly ever after. He was arrested within hours of his arboricide as he tried to pay the bill for a highly bloatful and gloatful dinner at the "22" Club in the Big City. Naturally, he went to prison, where he languishes to this day. But the charge was not, as you might imagine, tree-snatching or the like.

It seems that during the very moments when Happy Humphrey was oozing his way across the Kertuffel back yard, the magic tree was in the process of yet another permutation, which is to say, growing spell. This time it was en route from blooming fives to tens. In the darkness of his greed (a dramatic image), Happy Humphrey paid no heed. And so he axed the arbor in the midst of metamorphosis. All of which resulted in much embarrassment, not only for Happy Humphrey himself, when he vainly tried to tell his flabby side of the story, but for the general credibility gap as far as fables like this are concerned.

You see, all Happy Humphrey had in his hands at the time of arrest at the Club "22" were interim-type leaves, nocturnal notes, kind of funny money. And they arrested the fat man of felony for trying to fob off these dubious things on Sidney Smartbottom, club cashier. For Sid knew well—and the arresting agents whom he quickly called confirmed, with the little laugh sanctioned by law in these matters—that the U.S. Government does not print eight-dollar bills with the portrait of William Jennings Bryan, who never even got to be President!

So justice triumphed, as it sometimes can.

And from now on we all of us are better people for this experience. Certainly our respect for common vegetables has been strongly enhanced. And our faith in fables affirmed and renewed.

Also, spread the word that not only should swords be turned into plowshares, but cars should be turned into beans.

My next tale will concern blueberries.

Good-bye

73 74 75 10 9 8 7 6 5 4 3 2 1